The BOSTON MASSACRE Mystery

Dan Greenberg

GReaT S✱uRCe®
EDUCATION GROUP
A Division of Houghton Mifflin Company

Reading Advantage Authors
Laura Robb
James F. Baumann
Carol J. Fuhler
Joan Kindig

Project Manager
Ellen Sternhell

Editor
Jeri Cipriano

Design and Production
Preface, Inc.

Photography and Illustration
Front cover, interior art by C. B. Mordan, except p. 22 © Bettmann/Corbis

Copyright © 2005 by Great Source Education Group, a division of Houghton Mifflin Company. All rights reserved.

No part of this work may be reproduced or transmitted in any form or by any means, electronic or mechanical, including photocopying and recording, or by any information storage or retrieval system without the prior written permission of Great Source Education Group, unless such copying is expressly permitted by federal copyright law. Address inquiries to Permissions, Great Source Education Group, 181 Ballardvale Street, Wilmington, MA 01887.

Great Source® is a registered trademark of Houghton Mifflin Company.

Printed in the United States of America

International Standard Book Number: 0-669-51420-9

2 3 4 5 6 7 8 9 10 – RRDC – 09 08 07 06 05

CONTENTS

Author's Note: History and Mystery — 4

Chapter 1 — A Troubled Visitor — 7

Chapter 2 — Little Doggies — 14

Chapter 3 — Unhappy Boston — 22

Chapter 4 — The Note — 28

Chapter 5 — Dog at Work — 32

Chapter 6 — The Wigmaker's — 43

Chapter 7 — Late Supper — 52

Chapter 8 — Cruel Suspicions — 60

Chapter 9 — Box 44 — 70

Chapter 10 — No Evidence — 84

Chapter 11 — A Peck of Trouble — 91

Author's Note: History and Mystery

The book you are about to read is part history, part mystery. The history in this story is real. It focuses on a single, terrible moment in American history—the Boston Massacre.

The book's mystery centers on the very same massacre, but it is a made-up story. My aim in writing this story was to blend fact and fiction into an exciting yarn that was both fun to read and historically accurate.

The Boston Massacre took place on March 5, 1770. The facts of the case are clear. On a cold, spring night, a group of British soldiers shot and killed five colonists. Why did the soldiers do it? Well, that depended on whose side you listened to. The colonists said one thing. The soldiers said another.

Thrown into this clash was a young Boston lawyer named John Adams. In 1796, Adams would go on to become president of the United States. But in 1770, John Adams was still just a young man, who was faced with a very tough decision.

The Situation

By the mid-1700s, the American colonies had become a key part of the British Empire. Trade was booming. The colonists enjoyed a great deal of freedom. Most were loyal to the King of England.

This all changed in 1765 with something called the Stamp Act. The Stamp Act was the first of many steep taxes that were placed on the colonists by King George III. The purpose of these taxes was to pay off the king's war debts.

How did the colonists feel about paying for the king's wars? They didn't like it one bit. By 1769, a year before the massacre, colonial anger was about to boil over. That was when the king ordered British troops to Boston to "quiet things down."

Unfortunately, the troops did not quiet things down. Instead, the situation in Boston grew worse. Fights broke out between soldiers and citizens. More importantly, the poorly paid Redcoats (British soldiers) took jobs and houses that the colonists felt rightfully belonged to them.

Many colonists began to fight the British in any way they could. Secret groups like the Sons of Liberty rose up. Sam Adams (cousin of John Adams) and others established the Sons of Liberty to fight the British in a variety of ways. This secret group organized boycotts, protests, and disruptions. They would also tar and feather, or punish, British supporters (Tories) to keep them in line.

Mystery as History

By the spring of 1770, Boston was like a bomb ready to explode. It didn't take much to set off this bomb. On a narrow street, an argument started. Redcoat soldiers arrived. Shots were fired. The next morning, young John Adams was dragged into the case. Would he defend the soldiers in court?

As the story opens, try to imagine the situation that Adams faced. Keep in mind that the history and mystery of this story are blended together. Many of the characters, like **John Adams, Sam Adams, Paul Revere,** and **Abigail Adams,** were very real people. Others, like **Simon Doggett, Mr. Bunger,** and **Pleasant Princess Jones,** are fictional. Together, they make *The Boston Massacre Mystery* come to life.

CHAPTER 1

A Troubled Visitor

Boston, Massachusetts, March 6, 1770

My name is Simon Doggett. Folks call me "Big Dog"—first, because of my name, but also because I'm big, strong, and kind of dog-like in a way. I never give up once I sink my teeth into something.

Some folks think that because I'm big, I'm also dumb. All I can say is, that's a *big mistake*. You may be able to put one over on me for a while, but sooner or later, I'll sniff out the truth. And then you're in trouble.

I live in Boston and work for a lawyer named John Adams. Mr. Adams is as smart as I am big, as honest as I am strong. He's a man of words and ideas in the same way that I am a man of actions. Like myself, Mr. Adams has been around. He's wily and wise and pretty much knows every trick in the book. But was he ready for what came walking in that morning of March 6, 1770?

No one could have been ready for that.

So there we were on that cold morning, Mr. Adams at his desk, myself by the fire. I had my pocket knife out and was whittling a small, wooden dog. Suddenly, we heard a pounding at the door:

"Please! For the love of all that's good!"

A moment later, in bursts the most troubled man I've ever met. Forrest is his name, James Forrest. Tears are streaming down his cheeks.

"You've *got* to help them!" he cries.

Mr. Adams looks up from his book. "Help *whom*?" he asks, ever so calm.

Then out tumbles the story. Oh, we had already heard a good part of it by then. It was all over town. Words like TERRIBLE DEED! DREADFUL MASSACRE! were in the air. The Sons of Liberty were making sure everyone was properly horrified.

The bare bones of what happened are this. The night before, on King Street, five men were killed in cold blood by a group of nine British soldiers.

Mr. Adams, his partner Josiah Quincy, and I were all here in the office when it happened. We heard the fire bell, and we saw people running toward King Street at about nine o'clock. But none of us went down there. None of us saw anything.

Earlier this morning, Sam Adams had come around to talk about what they were already calling "The Boston Massacre." Sam is Mr. Adams's cousin. He is also one of the Sons of Liberty.

Who are these Sons of Liberty? Well, some folks call them traitors. But if being against unfair British taxes makes you a traitor, then I suppose lots of us are traitors, including Mr. Adams and myself.

You see, we've got what you call a "situation" here. When the king needed money to pay for his war, his ministers came up with a brilliant idea:

Tax the colonies!

And what happened when the colonies started to gripe about those taxes? The king sent troops here to Boston to "quiet us down." Of course, trying to put us down just made everyone even *madder* than they were before.

The only ones who really *do* something about all this injustice are a small, secret group called the Sons of Liberty. Sam Adams is one of their founders and main leaders.

"Five men gunned down in the street," Sam had told us earlier that morning. "You've got to admit, that's nothing to sneeze at."

It surely wasn't. No one was sneezing here. As far as Sam was concerned, this was the outrage he had been looking for, the spark that might lead all the way to Sam's ultimate goal: *revolution*.

But now here's Mr. Forrest, a merchant, telling us the other side, the Tory side, the British side.

"They're innocent!" he says, meaning the nine soldiers. "They didn't do it."

"How do you know?" Mr. Adams asks.

Forrest goes on with a jumble of facts, half-facts, and what I would call "wishful facts"—things he *hoped* to be true. He says nothing to convince either of us that those soldiers are innocent. But does that matter to Forrest? Not one bit.

"You *must* take this case!" he says to Mr. Adams. Tears once again well up in his eyes. He has been all over town. Mr. Adams, he claims, is his last chance for hope.

But what Mr. Forrest doesn't understand is that Mr. Adams has a position in this city, a reputation to keep up. He's a fine lawyer—the *best*, in my opinion. So why would he want to go and risk everything for a cause he doesn't even believe in, a cause he's against?

"That's just the point," Forrest says.

He explains that if some Tory lawyer stands up in court for the soldiers, what would folks think? That he's just some Tory lawyer.

And they wouldn't believe a word he says.

If, on the other hand, Mr. Adams stands up for these poor fellows, *that* would mean something. People will believe John Adams because—well, because he's John Adams. He's a straight shooter— an honest, plain-speaking man. So, in Forrest's mind, Mr. Adams is the only hope these soldiers have. Without him, they are doomed.

"Doomed!" Forrest keeps repeating, wagging a crooked finger at us.

Well. Mr. Adams looks over at me. I'm still whittling at my piece of wood. Normally, I would never dream of speaking at a time like this. After all, Mr. Adams is the lawyer here. I'm just the "muscles" of the operation (so to speak), not the brains.

But someone has to explain to Mr. Forrest one thing. Mr. Adams may not officially belong to the Sons of Liberty or even agree with half the things Sam Adams and his pals do. But make no mistake. Mr. John Adams is a patriot, through and through.

And then there's just the whole situation here. Ever since the British brought their two regiments to "quiet" things down, our normally gracious and courteous residents have been anything but gracious or courteous to their Redcoat "guests," frequently greeting them with such sentiments as,

"Get out of town, you lobster-backs!"

Does Mr. Forrest recognize just how much the folks around here *hate* these soldiers? They boss us around, take our jobs, and move into our houses, grabbing our money and food. And now, Mr. Forrest is asking Mr. John Adams to *defend* these fellows—these murdering soldiers who shot five people in cold blood?

"It's suicide," I say. "What you're asking Mr. Adams to do here is suicide, Mr. Forrest. It could destroy his career. It could destroy his whole life!"

"Now, now," Mr. Adams says, patting the poor man on the shoulder.

At this point, I figure we have given Forrest about all we can give. He has pleaded, we have listened, and there isn't much else we can do except send him on his way. This is when Mr. Adams says, "I'll take your case, Mr. Forrest."

"You'll *what?*" I say.

"You heard me, Mr. Forrest," Mr. Adams says. "I'll take your case. I'll defend Captain Preston and the other soldiers. You can count on me."

I can't believe my ears. I set down my whittling knife.

"Mr. Adams—" I begin.

But he stops me right there. The decision is made. Mr. Adams will defend the hated British soldiers.

Heaven help us all.

CHAPTER 2
Little Doggies

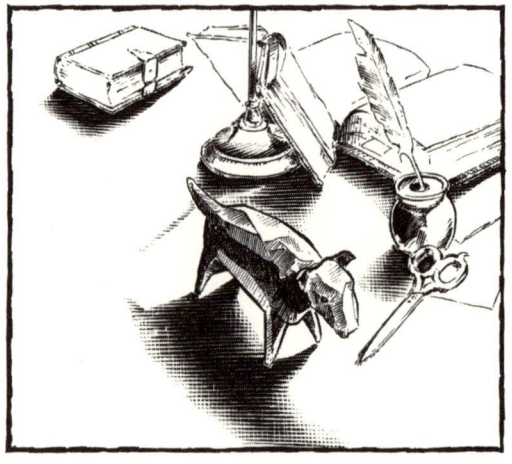

When Forrest finally leaves, the first thing Mr. Adams does is smack himself on the forehead.

"What have I done?" he groans.

To which I add, "And *why* have you done it?"

"That's easy," he says. He did it because, as Forrest said, it had to be done, and because no one else would do it. In other words, because it was his duty.

"Duty?" I ask. "Is it your duty to defend heartless scoundrels who murder people in the streets?"

"As a matter of fact," he says, "yes. You see, defending an honest sort is an easy decision. The more honest and righteous the prisoner is, the easier it is to be on his or her side.

"The real test comes in a case like this one, when the right and wrong of it are *not* so clear, when you need to search your heart and your soul to see your way through the fog.

"I would rather see five guilty people go free than one innocent person suffer unfairly," he tells me.

That's an interesting thought, but I remind him, "These fellows are killers—murderers!"

"And they don't deserve a strong defense just as much as anyone else?" he argues. "Are all people *not* created equal?"

"Hmm," I say. I can't really argue with that. If he thinks these killers deserve to be defended, then I guess that's his business. But how he is going to do it is another thing entirely.

"How *are* you going to do it?" I ask.

"That," he says, with a big grin, "is where you come in, Dog."

And so I am put to my task. In a nutshell, here is my mission: *find out everything that happened on the evening of March 5. Talk to everyone, hunt down every fact and detail, and leave no stone unturned.*

I set down my knife. Time to get to work.

Where to start? When in doubt, go to the source, I always say. In this case, that means starting at the Sheriff's Office, over in the Old Town House.

Sheriff Greenleaf is a friend of mine, but I can't get in to see him—not today. Old Barney, the sheriff's assistant, stops me at the front counter. I hand him one of my carved, wooden doggies, a gift.

"No time for nonsense today," Barney says, taking my gift without looking up. "Big doings in the city of Boston."

"Tell me about it," I say.

Gently, he sets the wooden doggie on his desk.

You see, these doggies I whittle aren't at all just for passing time. I give them out as favors, you might say, so folks like Old Barney might be more likely to "open some doors" for me (so to speak). At least, that's the idea. Give them a treat and they'll be your pal—or something like that.

Old Barney eyes the doggie and says, "Thank you kindly, Dog. This will make a fine gift for my niece Priscilla. But I still have no time for you—on account of the killings, you know."

"Ah, the killings!" I say, sensing an opening.

Barney puts a finger to his lips. "Not a word," he says. "Sheriff Greenleaf says we can't say anything to anyone about the killings. Besides, we haven't even copied all of the depositions yet. We haven't put together their statements."

I look at the papers on his desk. "Is that what you're working on?" I ask.

He nods. "Captain Preston's deposition," he says.

A deposition is an official statement made by a prisoner (or anyone else) about what happened. Captain Preston was the officer in charge over on King Street last night. His commander was Colonel Bradigan. The sheriff is holding Captain Preston and eight others—the soldiers we are defending—for possible murder.

I scan the document as fast as I can, catching a few odd phrases such as "... saw a great commotion," "... cruel and horrid threats," "... vengeance," and "... murder!"

"You mind if I—"

"I'm sorry, Dog," Old Barney interrupts. Then he says, "Thanks for the toy dog and everything, but you have got to get out of here. I have work to do. We all have work to do."

Barney stands up, ready to shoo me away, when suddenly the door to the sheriff's back office opens, and guess who walks out?

It's none other than Mr. Sam Adams himself.

"Dog!" he cries. "Fancy seeing you here."

Funny, I'm thinking the same thing about him.

"Walk with me over to Paul Revere's," he says. "I want to show you something there."

So out the door and into King Street we go, heading toward North Square. It's a cold and clear March morning with the crisp chill of winter still in the air. The great Sam Adams, leader of the Sons of Liberty, walks fast, and he talks fast, too. So before I can even begin to ask him what he was doing back there at the sheriff's office, he's asking *me* what *I* was doing there.

I don't think he's going to like this.

"You might as well know, your cousin John is representing Captain Preston and the other prisoners," I say.

Instead of exploding, Sam is silent for several steps, and then several more steps. Then he stops and looks me dead in the eye.

"They are guilty, you know," he says.

"That remains to be seen," I say.

"Not by my eyes," he says. "The evidence shows it, Doggie. I saw the depositions, and there is no doubt that they did it. They killed five men, and you can save us all time right now and tell that to good Cousin John. He's got no case!"

"You might be right," I say, "but that still doesn't mean they don't deserve a fair trial."

This stops Sam in his tracks once again. He eyeballs me, squinting.

"Is *that* what this is about?" he says. Then he slaps himself on the knee, laughing. "That John Adams is really something," he says. "Here we are, Revere and I, nearly killing ourselves to get these fellows put away, and what's old John worried about—whether or not they get a fair trial! I'm impressed, I really am."

Impressed? Frankly, I thought he might be furious with him.

"Does that mean you'll help us, Sam?" I ask.

"Help you?" he says, roaring with laughter. "Oh no, Dog, I'm not going to help you. I'm going to do my best to *destroy* you, or at least to destroy your case."

"Nothing personal," I say.

"Of course not," he says, clapping me on the shoulder. "You do what you have to do. It's as simple as that. I love my cousin John, but he is NOT going to win this case—not if I can help it!"

Here, he once again roars with laughter. We're in the North End now, and Revere's house is on the next block. I laugh along with him, though I'm not all that sure what I'm laughing about.

"You know," he says, "when you think about it, isn't that what this whole fight is really about? We're going to build a new America, Dog, and that's what we need to decide—what kind of place we want this to be. And here I agree with Cousin John. I want America to be a place where everyone gets a fair shake—everyone."

"Even British soldiers?" I ask.

He has to think about this one for a while. "Doggone it," he grins, "even British soldiers!"

We are at Paul Revere's house now. A gaggle of kids is playing out in the yard, both girls and boys. We go around back to Revere's silversmith shop.

"Wait until you see this," Sam Adams says.

CHAPTER 3

Unhappy Boston

Now, Paul Revere is just about the most charming man in all of Boston. He's handsome, strong, and a great talker—not to mention an artist, a politician, and a world-class silversmith and goldsmith. But as a leader of the Sons of Liberty, is Paul Revere also a man who would stretch the truth to help his own cause? This is something I'm still not sure about.

Right now we're standing in the shop, looking at Revere's latest handiwork. It's a drawing. He's actually going to turn the drawing into a color poster that he has given the title "The Bloody Massacre in King Street."

Once it's finished, he will etch the outlines of the drawing onto a special metal plate to make an engraving. Then he can ink the plate to make lots and lots of posters. He will send those posters out all over the countryside to every village, shop, and farm.

And what posters they will be!

Here's the setup. You see soldiers lined up on one side, muskets drawn. An officer stands tall behind them, giving the "Fire!" signal. Across the way, innocent citizens are dropping like flies. The guns are firing, smoke is billowing, and underneath, Revere has printed:

Unhappy BOSTON! See thy Sons deplore,
Thy hallowe'd Walks besmear'd with
Guiltless Gore!

Goodness!

"Is this what really happened?" I ask.

Mr. Sam Adams smiles sheepishly. Then he looks to Revere, before conveniently reminding him that I work for his cousin John.

"And Cousin John is defending Preston and the others," Sam explains.

Revere scratches his chin, thinking. "So I've heard," he says.

Again, the two hesitate, looking at one another, then back at me.

"Will someone please explain what is going on here?" I ask.

Revere puts his arm around my shoulder.

"What you need to understand," he says, "is that this is *war*, Dog. We're fighting a war here."

"Is that so?" I say. "If this is war, then where's our army? Where's our battlefield?"

"Our army?" Sam asks. "Look around you, Dog. Our army is everyone. It's you, it's me, and it's the butcher, the baker, and the candlestick maker. It's Mr. Paul Revere, Mr. John Adams, and Mr. Simon 'Big Dog' Doggett, by gosh!

"And our battlefield is everywhere, Dog. It's every bloody place where British oppression knocks us down. But mostly, it's right here in Boston. Boston is our battlefield, Dog."

Now this has been a fine little speech. I admire Sam's way with words quite a bit, to tell the truth, but it still doesn't answer the key question.

"Let me ask you both again," I say, pointing to the drawing. "Is this what really happened on King Street? Did the soldiers just mow them down?"

"Well," Sam says, "depends on who you talk to."

"Who did *you* talk to?" I ask.

"The sheriff," Sam says. "I also saw the depositions, and I spoke to some of the witnesses. They all said the same thing. Preston yelled, 'Fire!' So they fired, and they mowed them down, just like sitting ducks."

"Like sitting ducks," I repeated. "And what do the soldiers say about the situation?"

"Well," Sam begins. "As you can imagine, they have a different story to tell. They say that they are innocent. Of course, you and Cousin John would know more about that than either of us."

"Of course," I say. "And who do you believe?"

Paul cuts in here. "It's not that simple, Dog," he says. "It is not who we believe. It's what the city of Boston needs to hear and see right now."

"And you think the city of Boston needs to see *this*," I say, pointing to the poster.

"Exactly," Revere says, and both of the men nod at me.

I point out, "Didn't the shootings take place after nine o'clock at night?"

"Sure," says Sam. "What about it?"

"Well, this drawing shows a light sky," I say. "It makes it look like daytime."

Revere scratches his chin. "Hmm," he says. "Maybe you've got a point there."

Which makes me wonder how accurate the rest of it might be.

But this doesn't stop Sam Adams.

"Nonsense!" he blurts out. "You need to remember something here, Dog. Mr. Paul Revere here is an artist, and artists sometimes need to change or rearrange things for the sake of art. It's not a crime, you know."

"Maybe not," I say, letting the point go. But my mind is spinning. I'm thinking, *this is one case where an artist had better be pretty careful about getting things right. Otherwise, we all could be in a whole heap of trouble.*

The rest of my time at Revere's passes pleasantly enough. We sit in chairs, watching Revere and his apprentices work.

As Revere works, we talk about the case and about other things. Several kids run in and out. Revere seems to have an endless supply of them. He serves us a nice ale, which I take care not to drink too much of. After all, this case is only beginning, and I have a lot of work to do.

CHAPTER 4

The Note

STAY AWAY FROM THIS CASE

When I get back to Mr. John Adams's office, he is still gone. I figure he is probably at the jail, visiting the prisoners. So I pull up a chair and begin to sort some things out in my mind.

Three things seem to be clear. First, the soldiers did it. There seems to be no doubt about that. They shot those fellows, right there on King Street.

Second, if Revere's poster is any guide, the shootings were in cold blood. I mean, if you look at the drawing, there's no way around it. The soldiers line up on one side, and the defenseless citizens stand on the other. Bang! Bang! Bang!

Like sitting ducks. Like an execution.

My third conclusion seems to be even more obvious. This case is trouble, big trouble. From the way it looks now, there is no way to justify what those soldiers did. So how can Mr. Adams defend them? How could *anyone* defend them?

It's a good question. Fortunately, I don't need to wait to hear an answer. A few seconds later, Mr. Adams walks in through the door.

"Dog!" he says. "You're here. What did you find out?"

I give him a rundown: the sheriff's office, Sam and Paul, the massacre poster, and so on.

"I think we're in trouble," I tell him.

"You don't know the half of it," he says.

He tosses a small slip of paper in my lap. It's a note with a woodcut Jolly Roger—a skull-and-crossbones picture. (Pirate ships fly a flag with this same picture.) Across the bottom the note reads:

STAY AWAY FROM THIS CASE

Mercy! I take the paper in my hand. I notice that the words *are printed* on the page, not handwritten.

"When did—" I begin to ask.

"This morning," he says. "Under the door."

I bring the note to my nose. It's fresh ink and good thick paper, probably printed somewhere nearby.

"But who would—"

Mr. Adams stops me here. "Lots of people," he says. "Think about it, Dog."

He's right, of course. Who might have a reason to make a threat like that? Lots of people: revenge seekers, British-haters, and the friends or relatives of the fellows who were killed. That's just for starters. And then there are all those other outraged citizens who feel that "our" side needs to win, no matter what the cost. The list seems endless, almost, and the whole situation almost unreal. Yet, there it is, right in front of me. Someone has threatened the life of John Adams—and myself, for that matter.

"What does Abigail say?" I ask.

His face is grave. Abigail is John's wife, and you won't meet a finer, smarter, more courageous person than she.

I don't often say this out loud, but Abigail Adams is one of my true heroes. If even half of our leaders—or the British leaders—had half the good sense and wisdom of Abigail Adams, maybe then we all wouldn't be in such a mess. But they don't, which is why things at the moment *are* such a dreadful mess.

"I didn't tell her," Mr. Adams says. "I'm not going to tell her."

"Do you think that is wise?" I ask.

"I don't want to upset her," he says. "I'm not going to tell anyone about this, not even Josiah."

"Not your partner? Not even the sheriff?" I ask.

"I don't trust the sheriff," he says. "I don't trust anyone except you, Dog."

We both laugh. "I'm honored," I say. I know what's coming next: my new mission. Not only do I need to find out what happened on King Street that night, but now I also need to find out *who wrote that note? And, more importantly, why? And are they likely to back up their threat with action?*

"It's a tall order," Mr. Adams says, "but they don't call you the Big Dog for nothing."

"Hmm," I say. "I'll try to remember that."

But now it's time to get to work.

CHAPTER 5
Dog at Work

A good, sniffing dog generally locates its prey in three steps. First, you stumble and bumble around, sniffing everywhere and everything without much rhyme or reason. In Step Two, you start to narrow down your search. Then, finally, in Step Three, you lock onto your target and don't let up until you reach the prize, whatever that might be.

Right now, I'm still in the stumbling and bumbling stage. Before I start any serious sniffing, I've got to find out what really happened that night *before* the shooting. I have to learn, in fact, what happened before the mob even gathered.

So I go down to King Street and start snooping around. I meet dozens of people, and most of them are not at all helpful. But eventually I run into a man named Bob Ratch, who works at a place called Gray's Rope Walk. They make ropes at Gray's Rope Walk—cables, they call them, the kind of ropes they use on ships.

I give Ratch one of my whittled, wooden dogs.

"Thank you kindly," he says, not quite knowing what it is.

"Were you there?" I ask him, meaning at the massacre, of course. It turns out he was sleeping on the night of March 5.

"On account of the pain," Ratch says.

"What pain?" I ask.

Ratch explains, "It was three nights before the shooting," he says. "Here at the Rope Walk, the boys and me were out on the street corner, and along comes this British soldier. He sure was a handsome fellow and had a nice, red uniform with shiny buttons."

I listen to Ratch carefully because I'm not sure what he is leading up to.

"So I ask him, 'Looking for work, sir?'" Ratch explained. "I'm real polite, and when he shows interest, I move in closer. 'Out back,' I tell him. 'Go to the wooden outhouse. Go and clean it, sir, and I'll give you a penny!' Haw! Haw! Haw!"

Apparently, this is so hilarious that Ratch can't control himself. He starts laughing so hard he begins to cough. I have to wait several seconds to continue.

"So what happened?" I ask.

"Same soldier came back later," Ratch says, "with his Redcoat chums."

"You had a fight," I say.

He nods. "Bloody lobster-backs," he says, his face darkening with anger.

He shows me some of his "souvenirs" from the fight. He has gashes and bruises, scrapes and scratches. He is red and purple and black and blue. To dull the pain, he had a "wee bit" too much to drink on the following evening—and the evening after that. That was the night of the massacre. That's why he had been asleep.

"But you woke up," I say.

"Aye," he nods.

Ratch had woken up when all the commotion started and run out to where the soldiers were. But he was too late and didn't see much.

"Smoke," he says. "Confusion. There were folks running and yelling."

Ratch stops and points to a man through the window of the shop.

"See that fellow?" he says. "That's Curly Watson. He's got a wife and baby at home. Just last week, some lobster-back took Curly's job for less pay. The soldiers—they take the food right out of our mouths."

This doesn't quite make sense. If a British soldier took Curly's job, then why is Curly still working here now? Then I remember. Governor Hutchinson called all the British troops out of Boston to avoid trouble after the massacre. Every last Redcoat had left the city as of this afternoon.

So with the soldiers gone, old Curly must have gotten his old job back.

"Must be tough," I say.

"You don't know the half of it," Ratch says, spitting into the street.

As I take leave of Ratch and move down King Street, I try to keep folks like Curly Watson in mind. I can imagine how much they must hate those soldiers. Wouldn't you hate somebody who took away your job? I sure would.

I speak to a lot of other folks who have similar tales to tell. They were there, but they didn't see much, or they didn't quite understand what they saw. Most of the people heard the fire bell and came running, only to find it was all pretty much over by the time they got there. Some of them saw the blood and the commotion, and perhaps even bodies being hauled away. But few were there early enough to know what actually started it all.

I keep snooping until I happen upon a young woman behind the counter in a place called Bunger's Print Shop.

"Pleasant Princess Jones," she says, as I take her hand. "Pleased to make your acquaintance, kind sir."

"Simon Doggett," I say, placing one of my carved, wooden doggies on the countertop. "Folks call me Big Dog."

"Is this for me?" she says, as if I had just given her a diamond ring. Her eyes are dazzling, her smile is broad, and her voice is so musical that its total effect on me is almost dizzying. Of course, many young women seem to have this very same effect on me. But at least in one respect, this young woman is different: she is an African.

"Big Dog," she says. "That's a mighty funny name, Mr. Big Dog. You look more like a big BEAR to me!" She laughs. I can't help but join in. Then I point out that she's got a mighty funny name herself—Pleasant Princess.

She laughs again. "That's what you English folks always say!" she says.

"I guess that's so," I tell her. "We sometimes forget that many Africans got their real names taken away from them when they were brought to the New World as slaves."

"That's right," Pleasant Princess says to me. "I've got a cousin named Lord Charles the Good. Can you fancy that?"

This draws a big laugh from me. "Are you still a—?" I ask.

"A what?" she asks. "A *slave*? Oh goodness, no! I have been free ever since we left South Carolina when I was a young child. It's going on fifteen years now. My mama came here and worked for old Mr. Bunger until he went to retire on the farm. Now I work for young Mr. Bunger, here in the city. The Bungers have been good to me. They have been good to us."

"What do you do here?" I ask.

She tells me that she works for Mr. Bunger in this print shop doing odd chores, but it also looks like she does some of the typesetting. That's skilled work—and it should be high-paying work.

"I know how to read and write," the Pleasant Princess tells me. "My mama taught me, and old Mr. Bunger—he taught *her*. Old Mr. Bunger is a good man, a very good and kind man."

"How about young Mr. Bunger?" I ask.

She sighs, "He's the owner now." Then she adds, "He's got a lot of money."

Indeed, the shop seems well-equipped. "If I had to guess, I would say that Mr. Bunger did a fine business in this shop," I say.

"You can say that again," she replies.

Before I got the chance to repeat what I had just said about Mr. Bunger, a red-faced man comes storming into the print shop. He's a tall, pear-shaped fellow with a weak chin, and he's angry about something. He grabs Pleasant Princess by the arm, pulling her back.

"Princess!" he sneers. "You're wasting time! You're supposed to get that broadside ready by twelve noon, and it's going on eleven!"

"Ow!" she cries, cringing. "You're *hurting* me, Mr. Bunger!"

Suddenly, he looks up and notices me. I stare straight at him.

"Oh, sorry," he says sheepishly.

Then she tells him, "It's done, except for the bottom column." Once again, he takes her arm.

"Idiot!" he shouts. "How many times do I need to say it? *Finish* what you start! I need that whole thing done by twelve noon!"

She shakes away from him and says, "If you remember correctly, *sir*, you said that *you* would finish the bottom column yourself."

"I did?" Mr. Bunger says. "Oh, you're right. I did say that, didn't I? Hmmm, well, run along now, Princess. You have work to do."

The Princess goes to the back room, rubbing her arm, so now it's just Bunger and myself at the counter, standing there. I don't like this fellow, not one bit.

He shrugs, then smiles timidly. "These *people*," he says. "I don't know how many times I've said it. *They* take care of the work. *I'll* take care of the customers."

"I'm not a customer," I tell him.

Briefly, I explain who I am and that I'm working for a lawyer, trying to find out about the massacre. Suddenly, Bunger gets very busy, nervously fidgeting with the rows of metal letters behind the counter.

"Were you there?" I ask, meaning the massacre.

"Of course," he says.

"And?" I finally say.

"Shocking," he says. "Dreadful. Those troublemakers should all be locked up." At this point, the Princess returns, looking for a row of letters under the counter.

I'm a bit confused now. "Do you mean the soldiers or the citizens in the street should be locked up?" I ask.

"Oh no!" Bunger says. "I mean yes. That is, I believe that—"

The Princess butts in here.

"Mr. Bunger signed up to be one of the Liberty Boys!" she says.

Bunger's face reddens with rage. He's squeezing so hard on the type case he had picked up that his knuckles are turning white. But he pretends that nothing's the matter.

"Princess," he says, "why don't you let Mr. Doggley and me speak here alone."

"With pleasure!" the Princess says, once again returning to the back room.

When she's gone, he relaxes his grip on the type case. Then he takes a deep breath and shrugs once again.

"Sorry about that," he says. "I, uh—"

Clearly, he is worried about being identified as one of the Sons of Liberty, but I assure him that he can be straight with me. I have nothing against the Sons of Liberty. They may do "illegal" things, but it's no crime just to be a member of the group. At least, as far as I know.

"Yes, of course," says Bunger, still trying to look relaxed while he holds the type case.

From here on in, it's clear that I'm not going to get much out of him. He was at the massacre, he says. But he didn't see much. Or hear much. Or notice much. In fact, it makes me wonder whether he was really there or not. But it's hard to imagine why someone would lie about such a thing.

"Now if that's all, Mr. Doggley," he finally says, "I have a lot of work to do."

"It's Doggett," I say. "My name is *Doggett*, Mr. Bunger, not Doggley."

"Of course," he says, still holding that type case.

I head for the door. Just before I open it, I turn around. Bunger is watching me and still holding that type case. Then I remember what he said about finishing the column by noon. I wonder just what Bunger has in mind to write in that bottom column.

CHAPTER 6
The Wigmaker's

Since I didn't find out much at the Rope Walk or the Print Shop, I don't expect to learn much at the wigmaker's. But I'm wrong.

"My name is Doggett," I say, sitting down in the wigmaker's chair, hat in hand. The shop is not crowded. It has the sweet smell of fancy powders and expensive oils. Wigs made up in the latest London styles sit perched on stands.

Customers can buy wigs here made out of horsehair, goat hair, yak hair, or human hair. In the corner, a wealthy gentleman is having his hair oiled and dressed for the day. Two apprentices, Lucy and Brill, scurry over to me. They seem to be laughing about something.

"Is everything all right?" I ask.

"Sorry, sir," Lucy says. "It's just that—"

"What she means to say, sir, is that, well, we don't often get such a *simple* style to work with in here," Brill quickly explains.

Are they calling my hairstyle *simple*?

"Well, no," Brill giggles. "That is, actually, yes."

"What Brill means to say, sir, is that, to be completely honest, your hair *is* a mess," Lucy finally says. "It's an utter and total mess—style-wise, anyway."

"A tangle," Brill says, shaking his head sorrowfully. "A terrible tangle."

"And such a handsome gentleman, too!" Lucy adds cheerfully.

I ignore the comments about my hair and my looks. "I'm not here for my hair," I say. "I need information."

"Ah, sure," Brill says. "Of course, that's what all the gentlemen tell us. The men don't care a fig for how they look. Oh no! They are just here for—what did you say you're here for again, Mr. Doggett?"

"I need some information," I say, "about the massacre on the fifth of March."

Suddenly, Lucy and Brill's expressions turn serious.

"Ah, that," Lucy says sadly.

Before long, I realize I have stumbled upon two people who actually know what happened that day. They tell me that they know what started the incident. They tell me that it all actually *did* start right here, in this wig shop, with their friend Garrick.

"Who's Garrick?" I ask.

"Garrick is another apprentice wigmaker who works in this shop three days a week," explains Lucy. "He also works in another shop, so he is not here right now. Anyhow, on the evening of March 5, Garrick was standing outside the shop."

"Looking for trouble," Brill says.

I gather that neither one of these two has any great fondness for Garrick.

Anyhow, I find out that Garrick was out there when an army captain happened to walk by. And this wasn't just any army captain, either.

"This was a captain who owed our shop money," Brill says.

"For dressing his hair," Lucy adds. "Very elegant."

So Garrick called out, "When are you going to pay your bill, Captain, sir?"

The captain kept on walking, but a nearby sentry, whose name is White, overheard what Garrick said. So Sentry White went over to Garrick.

"You watch your mouth," White said to Garrick. "The captain is a gentleman. He will pay his bill at the proper time."

"Gentleman? Who is a gentleman?" Garrick replied in a nasty way to White. "Your regiment, sir, has no real gentlemen."

Sentry White clearly was not going to take such saucy talk about a captain from a lowly apprentice. White got *his* back up, so, of course, Garrick got his back up, too. They stood there, face to face, eyeball to eyeball.

"One thing led to another," Lucy tells me.

Push came to shove, and then shove came to—SLAP! White knocked Garrick down with his musket.

And then things really began to spin out of control. Garrick called for help. Onlookers gathered. Garrick was not badly hurt, but he was stunned. And he was bleeding. The onlookers soon swelled into a small crowd that surrounded White.

The crowd started jeering, "Bloody lobster-back! Go home!"

White had nowhere to turn. They were all around him, throwing all kinds of things. They threw ice, oyster shells, rocks, snowballs, and even rotten eggs. The shouting and jeering continued.

"Get out of town, you Redcoat!"

"Go back to Mother England!"

White thought that the crowd was mad enough to perhaps head for the Custom House, where the king's money was stored. So White yelled, "Call out the Main Guard!" The Main Guard was the troops that protected the Customs House.

At the same time, someone pulled the rope for the fire bell, and this sent dozens more people into the streets, thinking that there was a fire.

"I was one of those people who thought it was a fire," I tell Lucy and Brill. "Mr. Adams and I heard that bell from his office, but we didn't go over to King Street."

"You weren't looking for trouble," Brill says.

Someone got word to Captain Preston, who was in charge of the Main Guard. Captain Preston soon showed up with eight other soldiers. They all had guns in their hands.

The whole crowd gathered on King Street, and it became madness. Soldiers were on one side, citizens were on the other. Citizens were screaming, jeering, and throwing things at the soldiers. Citizens were daring them and taunting them. The soldiers just stood there stiff, not moving. They were afraid to move.

"Why don't you shoot, you darn cowards!" several folks cried out. But the soldiers just stood there like they were made of wood.

The only soldier who was moving was Captain Preston. He was in the back of the crowd, trying to keep things calm, trying to restore order.

Brill told me that it all might have blown over, had it not been for Attucks. That's Crispus Attucks, the black man.

"Did you know him?" I ask.

"A little," Brill says. "Big fellow. He was known around the wharf. Tough, he was, very rough and tumble."

"And Attucks came forward?" I continue to ask.

Lucy told me that it was a confusing situation. Some people say that Attucks grabbed the front soldier's gun. Others say that Attucks had a club. Either way, somehow it happened. The soldiers opened fire. There was smoke, screaming, people running, and blood.

The soldiers had fired upon "innocent" citizens. Crispus Attucks was the first to fall. Four others fell shortly after him.

"It was horrible," Lucy says, "simply horrible! I have nightmares about it, even now."

I agree that it did sound like a nightmare. I keep asking questions. But after a while, it appears that Lucy and Brill have told me about all there is to tell. I have just one more thing I need to know.

"At any point, did you ever hear Captain Preston yell 'Fire!' to his soldiers?" I ask.

Lucy and Brill look at one another.

"I heard *someone* yell 'Fire!'" Brill says.

"I didn't," Lucy says. "No one said so much as 'Boo.' They just fired on their own, and you know what? I don't blame them—not one bit."

I look over at Brill.

"I definitely heard something that *could* have been the word 'Fire!'" he says. "But I don't think it was the captain. I think it came from behind."

"Are you sure?" I ask.

"It was all very confusing," Brill says.

"And loud," Lucy says.

"And terrible," Brill says. "So terrible and shocking, I'm not sure of anything anymore."

When our interview finally comes to an end, they seem exhausted. They seem drained, as if telling about it made them relive the whole horrible experience.

I give them each a carved, wooden doggie for their trouble.

"Charming!" Brill exclaims.

"Before you go," Lucy says, "would you care to see some of our latest styles straight from London?"

I don't want to offend them, but I really can't see myself in one of those powdery things. I thank them but tell them that a wig is not for me.

"You're probably right," says Lucy. "Some men just don't look good in a wig."

"And I have the bad luck of being one of them," I say. But I was thinking to myself that it was really good luck. No wigs for me—no way, no how.

After thanking them again, I'm on my way. When I walk outside, I see that day has turned to night. The air is damp and raw. I don't waste any time getting back to Mr. Adams's office. I don't enjoy the weather, and I have much to tell Mr. Adams.

CHAPTER 7

Late Supper

When I get back to Mr. Adams's office, he is waiting for me. Abigail is there, too. The two of them are having a late supper in the office. Abigail is in from Braintree, where the Adams farm is. She has left the children with Mrs. Roche so she can spend a few days up here in Boston.

Mr. Adams tells me that he has been down at the station all day. He has interviewed witnesses and prisoners.

"My, my," Abigail says, as I sit down. "What have we here? It's Simon Doggett, lost dog, in from the cold."

"Lost and hungry," I say. "Do you mind if I—"

"By all means!" Mr. Adams says generously. "Help yourself, Dog."

So I dish out a bowl of stew and a fistful of still-warm biscuits.

"Well?" Mr. Adams says.

Abigail slaps him playfully on the wrist. "For goodness sakes, John," she says, "let the poor fellow eat his supper in peace."

But before long, I am well into it, describing my adventures during the day. I start with the Rope Walk and the fight between Ratch and the soldiers. It just shows how much bad blood there was between the locals and the Redcoats even *before* any of this happened.

"I also heard about the fight at the Rope Walk," Mr. Adams says. "Do you know who Private Matthew Killroy is?"

I shake my head.

"Killroy is one of the soldiers who's being held for shooting a man named Samuel Gray."

"So?" I ask.

I learn that Killroy and Samuel Gray were both at the same Rope Walk fight between the Redcoats and citizens that Ratch talked about. More importantly, Private Killroy was heard making threats at that time.

"To Gray?" I ask.

"To everyone, actually," Mr. Adams says.

"Killroy promised the citizens that if he ever so much as laid eyes on any of them again, they would pay. So then, a few days later, guess who ended up on King Street?"

"Gray and Killroy," I say.

"Gray was part of the mob that was harassing Sentry White. Killroy, on the other hand, was one of the soldiers sent to protect Sentry White. And Killroy ended up shooting Gray."

"Just like he promised," I say. "Unbelievable."

"It *is* unbelievable," Mr. Adams says. "But it happened—or at least, that's what the witnesses claim. At least *some* of the witnesses claim that."

"But how did Killroy know that Gray was out there in that crowd?" I ask.

"Killroy probably didn't know," Mr. Adams says. "It was probably just a coincidence. Dumb luck."

"More like bad luck," I say.

"You mean Killroy just fired," Abigail says, "and by chance he happened to hit Gray?"

Mr. Adams throws up his hands.

"Who knows?" he says. "Perhaps Killroy picked Gray out of the crowd, perhaps he didn't. The fact is we just don't know, and we'll probably never know."

"But that doesn't mean the prosecution won't use it against you," I say.

"They'll say it was revenge," Abigail says. "They'll claim that Killroy was making good on his threat, getting back at his enemy, Gray."

"You're right," Mr. Adams says, "they probably will do that."

"So what are you going to do, John?" Abigail asks.

Mr. Adams sighs. "I don't know," he says. Then he looks at me. "What else did you find out, Dog?"

I tell him what I learned at the wigmaker's. I tell him the whole story, starting with Garrick and ending with the soldiers firing. For several minutes, I talk and they listen. When I finish, Mr. Adams gets up and begins to pace the room.

"How does my story square with what the witnesses told you?" I ask him.

"It's pretty consistent," he says. "Even down to the part about whether or not Preston ordered his men to fire."

"What do you mean?" I ask.

"No one seems to tell the same story," Mr. Adams says. "Some witnesses swear they heard him yell 'Fire!' Others say he didn't. Still others say he yelled 'Fire!' not once, but three times. And then there are also those who say that it was *someone else* who yelled 'Fire!'—someone in the back, *not* Preston."

So my wigmaker apprentices, Lucy and Brill, were pretty typical. Lucy heard one thing, and Brill heard something different.

"It's actually quite normal and natural," Abigail says. "Different people hear and see different things."

To prove it, Abigail asks the three of us to hold up fingers to show how many biscuits I have just eaten.

Mr. Adams holds up five fingers, Abigail holds up four, and I could have sworn I ate no more than three of these delicious but not-very-large biscuits.

"You see!" Abigail says firmly and laughs.

We all laugh, but, of course, her point is well taken. How can anyone ever prove anything if every witness has a different story to tell?

"*You* don't have to prove anything," Abigail tells Mr. Adams. "A man is innocent until proven guilty. It's the other side that needs proof. If they can't prove what happened, your prisoners will go free."

"Hmm," Mr. Adams says. "That's true."

Of course, at this point, I'm curious about what Captain Preston had to say. After all, he was the commanding officer at the scene.

"Did you speak to him?" I ask Mr. Adams.

In fact, he spoke to Captain Preston for several hours. A few key facts emerged. First, Captain Preston's story was just as inconsistent as everyone else's was.

"Not that it's wrong," Mr. Adams says. "It's just that many of the details are different from the other witnesses'—and from the other prisoners'."

The second key fact Mr. Adams tells me is that Captain Preston insists that at no time did he ever order his men to fire.

"He swears it on his mother's life," Mr. Adams says. "And on *her* mother's life as well."

Mr. Adams adds that Captain Preston claims he never even told his men to load their guns, much less fire them. To avoid accidents, he ordered them to the scene with unloaded weapons. Only later did the muskets somehow get loaded.

Then I ask Mr. Adams, "What does Captain Preston say about all those who heard him give the order to fire?"

"Captain Preston claims that they are lying," Mr. Adams replies.

"Perhaps someone in the back yelled 'Fire!'" Abigail suggests.

"It's possible," Mr. Adams says.

I suggest that if Captain Preston had committed such a horrible act, why didn't he run afterward?

"Indeed," Mr. Adams adds. "Captain Preston had four hours between the end of the incident and his arrest. He easily could have escaped. Instead, he turned himself in, confident that he had committed no crime, that he had done no wrong."

"How about you?" I ask. "Are you confident that Captain Preston has done no wrong?"

Before Mr. Adams can answer this, something shocking happens.

CRASH!

The window breaks as something very hard and heavy comes smashing through. We hear hoofbeats and quickly run to the door. We open it and see a rider disappearing down the street. We can't see any detail of the person.

Mr. Adams closes the door and we walk back to where the object landed after it came in through the window. We discover that the object is a rock, and it has a piece of paper tied around it. We open the paper and see the same Jolly Roger skull-and-crossbones picture as we have seen before. The note on the paper says:

KEEP AWAY OR I WILL KILL YOU

"Oh, my word!" Abigail cries. "John?"

"It's all right, my dear," he says, trying to comfort her.

The cat's out of the bag now. And a very dangerous cat it is.

CHAPTER 8
Cruel Suspicions

Abigail, bless her heart, is more upset that Mr. Adams didn't *tell* her about the other threatening note than the note itself.

"I didn't want to worry you," Mr. Adams says.

"Worry me?" Abigail says. "You know what worries me? It's that my own husband wouldn't tell me when his life was threatened. That's what worries me, John."

"I'm sorry," Mr. Adams says. "I didn't know what you would say. I thought that maybe you would want me to quit the case, for the children's sake."

Her eyes are fiery now. "For the *children's sake!*" she cries. "I'm ashamed of you, John Adams. That's exactly why you can't *quit* this case. We must show that we don't back down. We must show that when some two-bit criminal makes a two-bit threat, we don't run. We fight!"

What did I tell you about Mrs. Abigail Adams? She's *something*, isn't she?

Anyhow, Mr. Adams apologizes, and we all go off to bed. Now normally, I doze off immediately, but tonight, something's eating away at me. At first, it's only a germ of an idea, but by the following morning, I'm certain of it. I think I know who's behind those threatening notes.

And I don't like it one bit.

The next morning, I get up, get dressed, and eat breakfast quickly. I must say that the flatcakes with sausage and the cider taste real good. I have a short exchange of words with Mr. Adams, and then I bid him and Abigail goodbye.

What I tell Mr. Adams is that I'm going to run down more leads on King Street today. I am going to do that. But, more importantly, I'm going to look into the doings of the one person none of us wants to suspect: Sam Adams.

Why Sam?

Why Sam, indeed! I guess my only answer to that question is *who else?* I mean, it could be anyone, of course. Anyone could have written those notes. But when you think about it, only Sam—or one of his buddies—has a real reason to make a threat like that. Oh, I'm not saying it was necessarily Sam himself. Perhaps he just suggested the idea to someone, or perhaps one of the Sons of Liberty did it on his own.

But one way or another, it stands to reason that the Sons of Liberty are the ones behind these notes. And like it or not, Sam is their leader, so Sam is responsible.

As Sam said to me the other day, "This is war."

And for him, it *is* war. Sam decided long ago that there is no dealing with the British reasonably. This is something that Mr. John Adams and I are not quite ready to admit yet. So we and Sam are hopelessly split. There is nothing left to discuss and no reason to hope.

For Sam, there is only one future for the colonies. There must be independence. And for that, we will have to fight.

Independence—now there's a word for you. It's a word that most of us don't dare even *think*, much less say out loud. But for Sam, it's the answer—the only answer.

While I don't agree with Sam completely on this matter, I don't completely disagree, either. Sam is at least partly right. Perhaps this really *is* war. Perhaps independence really is the only way to solve our problems. But again, folks like John Adams and myself are not ready to admit it—not yet, anyway.

Sam, on the other hand, has been fighting this war for a long time. And lately, his side has been losing. Oh, there was a big outrage over the Stamp Act. But that was five years ago, five *long* years. Other royal tax acts have come and gone. People get angry for a while, and then they forget.

But Sam doesn't want them to forget. He wants them all fired up. He wants them sizzling mad and ready to boil over.

And that's why this "Boston Massacre" was just what the colonists needed. Killing citizens in the streets—what could be worse? And you can bet that the Sons of Liberty plan to milk this thing for all they can get.

But what threatens them?

What if some lawyer—some talented, patriot lawyer like John Adams—were to stand up to defend the heartless, murdering soldiers? And what if he were to show that the soldiers were *not* such heartless murderers after all, and that it wasn't their fault? They were attacked by a mob, a crazed, out-of-control mob, and they fired only in self-defense. What if John Adams could prove all that?

In my mind, *that* is Sam Adams's biggest nightmare. So to prevent this nightmare from coming true, what has he done? He has threatened the lawyer—his own cousin—to STAY OFF THIS CASE.

I know that it's unbelievable. It's outrageous. I'm ashamed even to think it. Sam Adams is a good man, an honest man, and even a *great* man. He is certainly a man of principles. Would he or one of his friends be capable of doing something like this?

I honestly don't know.

At this point, I am reminded of Mr. Revere's poster. How easily it "stretched" the truth! It showed a light sky and broad daylight instead of dark night. It showed soldiers as attackers instead of peacekeepers. And the soldiers are firing on peaceful, innocent onlookers instead of an angry mob.

If Sam and his Sons of Liberty were capable of that, what else might they do? Again, I honestly don't know. And that's also why I don't want to say anything to Mr. Adams—at least not yet. I want to find out some things on my own first.

Two key clues seem to stand out. The first is that the message was not handwritten. It was printed on a printing press, using typeset letters and a woodcut image of a Jolly Roger.

Now, who has access to typeset letters and woodcuts? Paul Revere, of course. He does printing in his shop. He specializes in woodcuts, like the "Massacre" poster he was about to print up. The other person who comes to mind is young Mr. Bunger, the employer of Pleasant Princess. It's interesting that Princess blurted out that Mr. Bunger had recently become a member of the Sons of Liberty himself. Perhaps Bunger's first task was to print up a little note for Mr. Sam Adams?

I hope I'm wrong about all this. The thing is, they are not going to be obvious. Whoever did this will try to hide their effort. I can't just ask them, "Did you print this note?" So I need to be cagey. I need to somehow catch them in the act. But how do I do that? I'm just not sure yet.

I walk in the direction of Paul Revere's house. Again, Paul is more a silversmith than a printer, but he *does* print things—pamphlets, posters, and so on. On the way over there, I hatch a plan. If I go and talk to Paul directly, he'll know something is up.

So I decide to wait. I won't do any snooping until Paul is safely gone from his place. But how will I manage that? Luckily, it's a pleasant March day. The usual gang of kids is outside on the front lawn, playing in the melting snow.

I introduce myself to one of the oldest.

"Hi," I say. "What's your name?"

"Martha Anne Revere," she says. "Age nine."

"Hello, Martha Anne," I say. "Is your daddy at home?"

"I'm not sure," she says. "You want me to go out back to the shop and look?" She turns and begins to run.

"No, Martha Anne!" I cry. "Wait! Come back!"

She stops. When she returns, I explain to her that I have a surprise for her daddy. Her eyes widen.

"Oooh!" she cries. "I *love* surprises. What is it?"

I pull out one of my whittled doggies and show it to her. "Would you like one of these for yourself?" I ask.

"Oh *yes!*" she says.

So I recruit Martha Anne to "spy" on her own father, I'm ashamed to say. She peeks in on the shop and then comes back to me. Paul Revere is there all right, but he appears to be about to go out because he has his coat on. This is perfect.

After thanking Martha Anne and giving her the reward, I wait across the street behind a large oak. Sure enough, Revere comes out a few minutes later. As soon as he is safely out of sight, I go in.

"Simon Doggett," I say, introducing myself to Revere's apprentice, a young man I have never seen before.

"Henry Lee," says the apprentice with a smile, shaking my hand.

"Nice day out, isn't it?" I casually say.

We chat about the weather warming up, the melting snow, and how the kids love it all.

Now I feed him my story. I'm a man of science, I tell him, a friend of Ben Franklin's. (In fact, I actually *am* acquainted with Mr. Franklin, through Mr. Adams, of course.) I'm working on a new formula, a potion for killing rats.

Now the thing is, I need a printed label that clearly shows the potion to be poison.

"That's easy," Henry Lee says. "We can print you up labels that say POISON. How many do you want?"

"Actually, I wanted more than that," I say. "Since many of my customers can't read, I'll need a way of showing them that this liquid is poisonous so they won't go near it."

"Again, that's simple," Lee says. "Mr. Revere can just make you up a woodcut image in the shape of a Jolly Roger. A skull-and-crossbones picture signals 'poison' or 'danger.' That would do the trick."

"Would he need to *make* the woodcut?" I ask. "Don't you already have one on hand?"

"I'm not sure," Lee says. "I'll go check. But you're right. It would be less expensive if we already had the engraving. Less work for Mr. Revere."

So apprentice Henry Lee spends the next few minutes searching for woodcuts, going through the entire stock. The result is that he finds only one pre-made, skull-and-crossbones woodcut picture.

And even with the naked eye, I can tell it's not the right one. It's way too big to have printed the image on those two threatening notes.

My conclusion is that the notes were not printed in Paul Revere's shop. If they had been, Mr. Lee would have found the Jolly Roger woodcut that was the right size. So it seems quite clear to me that someone else printed the notes. I thank Mr. Lee and tell him I will soon get back to him with my order. Then, I am on my way.

CHAPTER 9
Box 44

The threatening notes were definitely not printed in Paul Revere's shop. So now I go to Bunger's Print Shop to see if he is responsible for printing the notes. Princess greets me as I enter the shop.

"Mr. Big Dog," she says with a welcoming smile. "You're back!"

She's hard at work, typesetting an advertisement for a local shoemaker. I look around and see that Mr. Bunger is nowhere in sight.

"I need to ask you a favor," I say to Princess. "I need you to look for a woodcut of a Jolly Roger, a skull-and-crossbones on it."

"You sure you don't want a dog?" she asks. "We've got some nice bulldogs that look just like you."

"No, thanks," I say. She goes to a rack on the wall that has numbered boxes. After a short search, she finds something on a high shelf.

"Here it is," she says, reaching toward the top. "Box 44, skull-and-crossbones."

She grabs a small box with the number 44 on the outside, but on the way down, something stops her. A hand grabs her by the wrist.

"Mr. Bunger!" she says.

"What are you doing with that?" he demands.

"*This*?" she says. "I was just . . . " She looks over at me.

"What's *he* doing here?" he asks.

Before she can even say anything, he stops her.

"I don't want to hear it!" Bunger snorts angrily. "You get back to work, Princess!"

Bunger takes Box 44 and stuffs it into his pocket. Then he turns to me. "And as for *you*—you get out of my shop, sir! I know what you're doing here, and let me tell you that I don't like it one bit!"

Now I have to tell you, a big yard dog like myself could pretty much gobble up a snappy, little lap dog like Mr. Bunger if I wanted to. But sometimes it's better not to fight—or, at least, to wait until the proper time.

I spend the afternoon across the street in the Green Dragon Inn, drinking cider and tea and waiting. Sooner or later, one of them is bound to come out of the shop. And sure enough, at around three o'clock, Princess comes walking out.

"Mr. Dog!" she cries, when she sees me on the walkway. She's carrying a basket, on her way to get charcoal for the stove fire. "What are you doing here?"

"I need to see that woodcut," I say. "Box 44."

Her eyes widen. "Oh, no," she says. "Mr. Bunger told me *never* to let you in the shop again. He's likely to kill me if I do. What's this all about, anyway?"

Briefly, I try to explain without giving too much away. For the most part, I ask her to trust me—for now, anyway.

She smiles. "You remind me of old Mr. Bunger," she says.

"Is that a good thing or a bad thing?" I ask.

"Good," she replies.

Then I lay out my plan. It's kind of risky, but there doesn't seem to be any other way. I need to get my hands on that woodcut.

Hours later, I'm still across the street at the Green Dragon, waiting for Bunger's Print Shop to close. I sit by the window, watching as Mr. Bunger locks the front door. When he leaves, it looks like he's headed this way. Quickly, I pay my bill and duck out the side door, hiding my face behind my coat. Then I walk around the block to the back entrance of the Print Shop. Princess is waiting for me there.

"Over here, Mr. Dog," she calls out softly.

Suddenly, I'm having second thoughts. This could get her in a lot of trouble. "Maybe we shouldn't do this," I say. "You could lose your job."

"It's all right," she says, opening the back door. "I don't like my job. I don't like Mr. Bunger."

"Neither do I," I say.

We stumble our way through the back entrance. It's dark and dusty in there and smells of ink. My plan is to make our way to the front counter and the shelves where the woodcuts are kept. But it's so dark that I can't see which way to go.

"Maybe we should light a candle," I say.

She shakes her head. "Mr. Bunger often eats supper right across the street at the Green Dragon," she says. "He could spot us through the window."

"Hmm," I say.

We stumble on a bit farther. "Look out!" I cry, knocking into a table, causing a stack of boxes to crash to the ground.

We wait. Did anyone hear us? The boards creak. Mice scurry in the walls and something rattles. Is it the wind? I take another step and knock into a crate.

That does it. I realize that we will never find anything in here unless we light a candle. So I convince Princess to strike a match.

With a small candle in hand, it's now an easy task to find our way to the front counter. We look around. Over to the right are the shelves that store the woodcuts, organized in numbered boxes. I hold the candle while Princess searches.

"It's not here!" she cries.

Sure enough, we find Box 42, Box 43, then Box 45 and Box 46. But there is no Box 44.

"Now what?" Princess asks.

"We have got to find that box," I say.

We look everywhere, checking all of the shelves, drawers, racks, and bins. We check the supply room, and I even spend a long time sorting through the trash. Box 44 is nowhere to be found.

"Maybe he took it with him," she says.

I remember that the last time I saw Bunger, he had stuffed Box 44 in the pocket of his smock. Maybe he just left it there. We look for the smock and find it hanging on a peg in the next room. But there is no Box 44 in the pocket.

However, I do find something interesting in the pocket. It's a slip of paper with the number 44 on it.

Now it's clear. This paper I just found is the old label for Box 44. Mr. Bunger must have taken out the woodcut and relabeled it with a new number, so nobody could recognize it.

"Does Mr. Bunger keep a list of all the numbered woodcuts?" I ask.

"In the drawer," she says.

There are 227 boxes in all on the list. Box 44 is the only one listed as a Jolly Roger. It's also the only box missing. It seems clear that the woodcut must be here. He just changed the number on the box so no one could find it. So now all we need to do is sort through all 227 boxes on the shelves.

"This could take all night," I say.

"Maybe not," Princess says, reaching for the final box at the end of the shelf. "Box 228," she says. "The label on this one is new."

Inside, we find a woodcut wrapped in a small slip of paper. I stuff the paper into my pocket and hold the woodcut up to the candle.

Bingo!

"It's a Jolly Roger, all right," I say.

Is it the *right* Jolly Roger? It seems to be about the right size and shape, but only time will tell.

"I'll need to take it home and match it to the notes Mr. Adams got," I say.

I hear a click. "I'm afraid you won't be doing that," a voice says.

"Mr. Bunger!" Pleasant Princess shrieks.

In the dim candlelight, I can see the cruel expression on his face. I can also see that he is holding a pistol.

"And don't think I won't use this!" he warns.

"But how did you—" the Princess begins.

"I saw you meet with Mr. Doggett this afternoon in the street," he says to Princess. "So I figured something was up. Bad idea to break in here, Princess, very bad!"

"Okay," I say, setting the candle on the counter. "You've caught me, Mr. Bunger. I confess. I work for a printer named Paul Revere. We heard you had some excellent woodcuts in this shop, so I came to get a look at a few of them. Nothing more."

"Nice try, Mr. Doggett," he sneers. "I know who you are. You work for that lawyer, John Adams, and you're here to cause trouble. So I'll take that woodcut from you—RIGHT NOW!"

He yanks the woodcut out of my hand and slams it on the counter. Then, still holding the pistol, he takes a hammer from under the counter and smashes the woodcut to pieces.

"Too bad, Mr. Doggett!" he laughs. "Your precious woodcut is now gone. It no longer exists."

Bunger thinks it's too bad, but he's wrong. Now we know for sure that it *was* Mr. Bunger who sent the notes. Why else would he smash the woodcut, the only evidence that could link him to the notes?

"*You* sent the notes to Mr. Adams!" I say in a raised voice to Bunger.

"And what if I did?" Bunger says, tossing the hammer to the floor. "You can't prove it now, not without that woodcut."

He's right, of course, but I'll never admit it.

"What if we call the sheriff?" I suggest.

He smiles. "Go right ahead," he says. "I'll tell him you broke into my shop. And Princess will back up my story—every word I say, or she'll lose her job. And I'll have her and her dear mother sent back to where they came from—the plantation in South Carolina."

"You wouldn't," I say.

"Oh, yes, I would!" he says, laughing gleefully.

In the dim light, Princess's eyes burn with anger. "You know what, Mr. Bunger?" she says. "I quit. What do you think of that?"

"You can't quit!" he cries. "You're a woman, a former slave. Where would you *ever* find another job?"

"I don't know," she says, "but I still quit, Mr. Bunger. I can't work for you. You're not like your father at all. You're a bad man, a *very* bad man!"

Bunger scratches his chin, smiling. "So I've heard," he says. "On the other hand, I just might shoot both of you right here and now. It would be self-defense, you know, just like the soldiers. What do you think, Mr. Doggett? Could your Mr. Adams convince a jury I was innocent in such a case?"

"I would rather be shot than have my mama go back to South Carolina," Princess says.

Bunger laughs. "Well, that's just too bad," he says. "I think you're going to like being in South Carolina again, Princess. I hear it's warm down there." Then he turns the gun toward me. "And as for you—"

"Wait," I say. "Before you do anything, Mr. Bunger, you at least owe me an explanation. What are you so afraid of? It's no crime—at least officially—to be a member of the Sons of Liberty."

"The Sons of Liberty?" he says. "That's exactly who I am afraid of, you fool. Don't you see the position I'm in, Mr. Doggett? I never wanted to join up with that gang of traitors and criminals in the first place. It was Colonel Bradigan's idea."

"Colonel Bradigan?" I ask. "You were working for the British commander?"

"Yes," he says. "My job was to report the plans of the Sons of Liberty to Colonel Bradigan."

"Ah!" I shout. "So, you're a traitor!"

Bunger laughs. "Me, a traitor? Think again, Mr. Doggett. Last I looked, we are all British subjects here. No, it's *you*, you and your Sons of Liberty friends who are the traitors. I went to those meetings with Sam Adams and the rest. They're fools, I tell you! Fools! They should be hanged from the nearest tree—the whole lot of them!"

He lowers the gun. But I'm still afraid that he might use it.

"So, you made a deal," I say. "You reported to Colonel Bradigan on what the Sons of Liberty were doing, in exchange for what? Money?"

"My father was a good man," Bunger says, "but when he ran this shop, he didn't make much money. Too nice, he was. When I took over, I found a way to make much more by doing jobs for the British and the Tories. But then, your Sons of Liberty began using tar balls. This was threatening my business!"

"Tar balls?" Princess says.

I explain to her that a tar ball is a glob of hot tar and feathers. The Sons of Liberty had taken to leaving these globs on the doorsteps of merchants who support or do business with the Tories, so that customers would avoid them.

Princess grins at me. She has no problem with what the Sons of Liberty are doing.

I turn to Bunger and tell him that the tar balls are a kind of message and that he could be next. This puts Bunger in a real bind. If the Sons of Liberty find out how much business he has been doing with the Tories and the British, he'll get tarred and feathered for sure. On the other hand, the British are his best customers. So if he stops trading with them, he won't be able to make a living anymore.

For a moment there, I almost feel bad for him. Then I remember Paul Revere and all the other printers in town. These men seem to get by without working for the British. So Bunger isn't trapped. He's just greedy.

"How much does Colonel Bradigan pay you?" I ask.

"Enough," he says, with an evil grin.

But that still doesn't explain why he sent Mr. Adams the threatening notes. Then it becomes clear. Bunger didn't report directly to Colonel Bradigan. Instead, he gave his information on the Sons of Liberty to somebody lower down on the chain of command.

"Captain Preston!" I cry.

He nods. Bunger usually brought his information to Captain Preston, who then reported to Colonel Bradigan. And that's where he was on the night of March 5. Bunger was in the act of visiting Captain Preston to give him information about the Sons of Liberty to pass on to Colonel Bradigan.

Suddenly, they were interrupted by the news on King Street. The sentry was trapped!

So now it all makes sense. Bunger didn't really care if Mr. Adams defended the soldiers or not. He just didn't want anyone—like me—snooping around the case. If we found out what Bunger was *actually* doing that night—working for the British, he would get tarred and feathered for sure!

"And I would be ruined!" Bunger adds. "So you'll have to forgive me, Mr. Doggett. You see, I'm in a rather desperate situation, here."

Now, I don't pretend to understand exactly what happens next. Let's just say that locked up inside of every Big Dog is a big, mean dog, a big, *mean* dog, who is just waiting to get out.

So I let him out.

I look at Princess and she looks at me. Poor Mr. Bunger, never even had a chance.

"Dunh!" he moans as we both plow into him.

That's right, both of us! Princess hits him high, and I hit him low. The gun misfires, the candle blows out, and Mr. Bunger drops to the floor like a sack of rotten potatoes.

A few moments later, we are ready to emerge from the shop. We have Bunger by the scruff of the neck, dragging him out the door. We march over to the sheriff's office, only to receive the surprise of our lives.

CHAPTER 10
No Evidence

"I'm sorry, Dog. There isn't a thing I can do," the sheriff says. "You know that I like you, son. But I can't let you out of here, not without evidence."

I still can't believe this. A man holds a gun on us. He almost kills us, and what does the sheriff—my friend the sheriff—do?

He locks us up.

"You don't understand," I say. "*We're* the victims here, not Mr. Bunger."

"Not according to the law," the sheriff says. "He says that you broke into his shop, and you admit it, Dog. So I have no choice but to hold you both for breaking and entering. That's the law."

"You just wait until Mr. Adams gets here," I say. "He'll get us out. He'll explain everything."

Mr. Adams does arrive shortly thereafter, with Abigail, but there's not much he can say or do.

"It's your word against his, Dog," he tells me.

The thing is, we don't have the woodcut. And without the woodcut, my whole story sort of falls apart. It's not that Mr. Adams doesn't try. He explains the situation to Sheriff Greenleaf. He shows the sheriff the threatening notes and even convinces him that the only reason we broke into the print shop in the first place was to find evidence to back up our case.

"It all makes sense," the sheriff says. "And I would like to believe you, Mr. Adams. But where is the woodcut with the Jolly Roger?"

"But that's just it," I say. "Mr. Bunger here destroyed the woodcut. He broke it into pieces with a hammer."

The sheriff shakes his head. "Sorry," he says. "Without evidence, you have no case, Mr. Adams. I'm afraid I'm going to have to release Mr. Bunger and hold these two for breaking and entering."

Bunger cackles as the sheriff opens the door to his cell.

"Sweet dreams, Mr. Doggett," he says to me. And then he turns to Princess. "And as for *you*, I'll see about South Carolina tomorrow!"

Princess's eyes darken with hatred.

"You won't get away with this, Bunger!" I cry.

"Watch me!" Bunger yells back gleefully, as he heads toward the door.

"Pipe down, Dog," says the sheriff. "There will be no threats made inside of this jailhouse. You are in enough trouble as it is."

So that's where it stands. The two of us are locked up. Mr. Bunger is set free. And John Adams, the finest lawyer in Boston, is powerless to do anything about it.

"Isn't there *something* you can do, John?" Abigail asks.

Mr. Adams shakes his head. "We will come in tomorrow morning to pay your bail," he tells me.

So we sit. As time passes, our predicament seems only to get worse. Princess, for the most part, seems sad about the whole thing and maybe a bit scared. I'm mostly just angry. And then by some odd chance, I reach into my pants pocket, and something crinkles.

I feel inside. It's the paper I took from Box 44 that was wrapped around the woodcut. I unfold it and quickly see that it appears to be a sample—a sample picture stamp from the Box 44 woodcut.

"Oh, my gosh!" I cry. "Sheriff! Come quick!"

It takes some doing, but I finally convince the sheriff to send a deputy out to get Mr. Adams.

"At this late hour," the deputy asks, "what should I tell him?"

"Tell him that I have something that will bust this case wide open!" I exclaim.

That's what I'm hoping, anyway.

Some minutes later, Mr. Adams once again stands in the doorway of the sheriff's office. It's late, and it must be raining again outside. He looks like a scrawny, wet cat standing there in front of us.

"What is it, Dog?" he says to me.

"It's a sample picture stamp," I say, "of the Jolly Roger that Bunger used to make the notes."

"What do you mean?" he asks.

I explain that I found the stamp in Bunger's shop, in Box 44, wrapped around the now-broken Jolly Roger woodcut. It's clear that the stamp was made as a sample to show what the woodcut picture would look like once it was stamped on a page.

It's also clear where the stamp came from. That's because BUNGER'S PRINT SHOP BOX 44 is printed in small letters across the bottom of the paper.

Mr. Adams takes out one of the notes he received and lines it up with the sample—Jolly Roger to Jolly Roger. And what do you know? It's a perfect match!

"Do you know what this means?" Mr. Adams asks.

"We're getting out of jail?" Princess asks hopefully.

"Better than that," I say. "We're getting out and Mr. Bunger is going in. We've GOT him, isn't that right, Sheriff Greenleaf?"

"I expect so," the sheriff says.

By the time we are released, the sheriff has already sent out two deputies to get Mr. Bunger. Now *he* has to face the evidence. He arrives some minutes later, boiling mad.

"This is an outrage!" he cries. "How dare you interrupt me at this late hour, Sheriff Greenleaf!"

"I expect that I'll be interrupting more than that soon enough," the sheriff says.

"What do you mean by that?" Bunger asks.

We show him the evidence—the threatening notes and the sample stamp from Box 44. There is no denying it. The Jolly Roger images are *identical*. This proves that the threatening notes were printed in Bunger's Print Shop.

"It may have come from my shop," Bunger says. "But you have no proof that *I* was the one who printed it."

Mr. Adams chuckles. "Come, come, Mr. Bunger," he says. "You think anyone is going to believe you, given that we now know you were working for Colonel Bradigan and the British?"

Bunger's face reddens. We've got him, and he knows it. He looks down at the floor.

Then he surprises us. I wouldn't have thought Mr. Bunger to be the type to make a mad dash toward the door. I wouldn't have thought that such a soft-looking fellow could move with such a burst of speed. He would have escaped right out the door of the sheriff's office, except for one small thing.

A foot stuck out at the last possible instant. The foot belonged to Pleasant Princess.

DONK!

Bunger trips over her shoe, then crashes to the floor in a spectacular, rolling heap.

"Nice move!" I say to Princess.

"Why, thank you," she says, grinning. "It was my pleasure!"

Meanwhile, Sheriff Greenleaf gathers Mr. Bunger up in an armlock. It is clear that Bunger won't be going anywhere for quite some time.

CHAPTER 11
A Peck of Trouble

To make a long story considerably shorter, here's what happens. The sheriff, with this new evidence, now has reason to lock up Mr. Bunger. So he does. The charge is conspiracy to commit murder. It so happens that it's a crime in Massachusetts to write threatening notes, especially if those notes threaten to kill someone.

Bunger, being basically a fool, howls like a sick tomcat as the sheriff loads him into a jail cell. "Get me out of here! Get me out of here!" Bunger keeps shouting.

There will be no such luck for him. They'll get him a lawyer tomorrow, I'm sure. I don't think Mr. Adams will volunteer—not for this case, anyway.

Meanwhile, the four of us head on home for a late supper. And who happens to show up, midway through our meal? It's none other than Mr. Sam Adams himself!

"Cousin!" Sam says to Mr. Adams. "Heard you were in a peck of trouble!"

"You heard right!" Mr. Adams says.

We have Sam pull up a chair and fill him in on everything that happened. Then we celebrate around the fire with cider and music. Mr. John Adams plays the violin while the rest of us sing. Abigail's fine, strong voice goes well with Sam's hearty baritone and is a good counterpoint to my own slightly off-key, dog howl. And Pleasant Princess does a superb job at the harmonica, which her daddy had taught her. All in all, we make some pretty good music.

As we sit there, singing and grinning, I can't help but look over at Sam. The thing is, when I said we told him everything that happened, I didn't mean *everything*. I believe in being honest. But I don't have the heart to reveal how I felt about Sam just a short while ago. I can't tell him I had suspected *him*, or one of his Sons of Liberty pals, of writing those threatening notes to Mr. Adams.

It's amazing what can happen in a day. Just this morning, I was convinced that Sam Adams—*our* Sam Adams—was a man who would threaten his own cousin and betray his own cause by lying and cheating. I can't blame myself for that. After all, Sam often says, "Anything for liberty!"

Looking at Sam, I think, *do anything for liberty? Well, perhaps not. Someday I'll make it up to you, Sam Adams, for thinking badly about you.*

And perhaps I will. But for now, Mr. Adams and I have a lot of work to do.

December 18, 1770

Mr. John Adams, his partner Josiah Quincy, and I have indeed had a lot of work to do over the past year. It's been almost nine months since that fateful morning when Mr. Forrest came banging on our door. None of us have been quite the same since.

What took place with Mr. Bunger is now just a small and distant memory compared to the matter of *the case*, the Boston Massacre, as it has come to be famously known up and down this land. In the bigger scheme of things, what happens to Mr. Bunger, or me, or even Mr. Adams is nothing compared to the importance of the case because this case involves the future of America.

So what has happened? Well, after a great deal of back and forth, Mr. Adams finally did represent Captain Preston in court just two months ago in October. The prosecution paraded dozens of witnesses in and out of the courtroom. As I have already described, each had a different story to tell. Some stories were just a little bit different. Some were wildly different.

But the overall effect was clear. In the end, no one knows what *really* happened on that fateful night of March 5, 1770. Perhaps Captain Preston gave the order to fire. Perhaps he didn't. Perhaps the soldiers fired in self-defense. Perhaps they didn't.

And so on. Was it an angry mob or an innocent gathering? No one can say for sure. Did Killroy shoot Mr. Gray? Perhaps; then again, perhaps not.

In the end, without any clear evidence one way or another, there was really only one verdict for Captain Preston that the jury could honestly reach: *not guilty.* After all, you can't send a man to prison if you aren't *absolutely* sure he committed the crime.

Pretty much the same thing happened a few weeks later during the second trial for six of the eight soldiers. Six of the eight were judged *not guilty.* The other two received manslaughter sentences. This makes sense when you figure that they really did kill five people.

Was justice served? Mr. Adams and I think so. But do we know for sure? No one knows for sure.

What we *do* know for sure is that, thanks mainly to one man—John Adams—we showed what kind of people we are. Oh, sure, he could have taken the easy way out. Mr. Adams could have refused to represent those soldiers.

"Not me!" he could have said to Mr. Forrest that day back in March. *"Let someone else do it."*

I can't tell you how much grief he got from the townspeople of Boston over the next few months. There were the looks. There were threats and names: *traitor, coward, double-crosser,* and worse.

But that's the thing about being in this country. Somehow, once you have lived for a spell in this land of freedom, it begins to change who you are and the way you think. I can't describe it, really. But, looking back, I somehow think that the Boston Massacre trials were the strongest message we ever could have sent to King George.

I mean, sure, we could have expressed our need for liberty by fighting. Fighting is sometimes necessary. Hey, it may still come to that here. Sooner or later, we may end up fighting a war with the British. But with those two trials, John Adams showed that we also cared about something *other* than fighting, something more noble and grand. And that's the idea that *liberty isn't just about being free to do whatever you like. It's also about respecting the freedom of others—even people you don't like . . . even British soldiers.*

And that's what Mr. Adams did when he took on that case and when he represented those soldiers so brilliantly in court. He showed King George and the rest of the world that there was another way—a *peaceful* way—to do things.

He showed that none of us are free unless we are *all* free. And that's a pretty important idea, when you think about it.